W9-BNJ-562

The Adventures of
Willy Nilly & Thumper

Book Three: Stella Star

Stella Star

By Jim Henry

with Jimmy Patterson

Illustrated by Marjorie van Heerden

willy nilly stories llc

The night settled like a warm blanket over Hoop 'n' Holler, and the town's famous best friends, Willy Nilly and Thumper, were toasting marshmallows. The blue-orange flames covered Thumper's treat.

"Thumper, why do you have to ruin a perfectly good marshmallow like that?" Willy Nilly asked.

"It's not ruined! When it's black, the gooey stuff in the middle is really yummy. That's when marshmallows taste best," Thumper said.

"I think they're better when they're brown on the outside and warm in the middle," Willy Nilly said.

The friends looked up at the sky, which overflowed with stars.

"Hey look, Thump," Willy Nilly said. "It's Canis Major."

"What's Canis Major?"

"It's one of the dog constellations," Willy Nilly said.

"Do you think there's a rabbit constellation up there somewhere?"

"Sure there is," Willy Nilly said. "It's called Lepus, and it's right in front of Canis Major."

A huge and particularly bright star cut right through the sky. It didn't seem to be burning out, but instead headed straight toward them.

"Hey Willy, how do you move out of the way of a falling star?"

"As fast as you can!!" Willy Nilly said. "Run!"

The star dropped below a grove of nearby trees. Tree limbs snapped and cracked. There was a very loud thud, and the ground shook.

"Let's go have a look," Thumper said.

"I can feel the heat," Willy Nilly said. "We have to be careful!"

Thumper agreed, but he rushed ahead anyway, fascinated. The two friends looked through the trees and saw a large crater.

The ground creaked, and the air was thick with dust and smoke, but they both saw something move inside the giant hole.

"It looks like a person!" Thumper said.

The two friends moved closer to investigate. It was a girl! And she glowed with a mysterious light.

She had pushed herself up into a sitting position and was leaning back against one hand. With the other, she brushed ashes and specks of space dust from her head and shoulders. She looked a bit shocked but gave a slight smile when she spotted a dog and rabbit in front of her.

"Are you okay?" Willy Nilly asked.

She nodded yes, then shook her head no, then nodded yes again.

"My name is Willy Nilly. This is my best friend, Thumper. What can we do to help you?"

The young girl shrugged, still appearing dazed.

"Here, have some water," Willy Nilly said, and handed her a bottle.

She took a long drink. "Thank you," she said. "There's nothing better than cold water after a space flight."

"So, are you a star?" Thumper asked.

"Yes. I'm Stella. Stella Star," she replied.

"Wow!" Thumper said.

"Are you hurt?" Willy Nilly asked.

"I'm a bit scratched up, and landing knocked the breath out of me."

"How fast do you think you were going?" Willy Nilly asked.

"I don't know. I think probably as fast as the speed of light."

"That's 186,000 miles per second," Willy Nilly said.

"I've always wanted to go that fast," Thumper said.

"Trust me, you don't want to do that. It's hard even on us stars. Where am I, by the way?" Stella asked.

"Hoop 'n' Holler," Thumper said. The girl looked confused.

"It's a town in Choco," Willy Nilly added. That didn't help either.

"Choco is a country. We're on Earth. You know . . . the *planet*?" Thumper said.

"Oh! Earth! That's right! One of you made a wish to see a star up close. I'm here to make that wish come true."

"It was me! It was me!" Thumper said, hopping up and down with excitement. "I wished on the first star I saw!"

Willy Nilly looked at him, puzzled.

Thumper explained, "You know how when you see the first star, you say the rhyme that goes like this?

Star light, star bright,
First star I see tonight,
I wish I may, I wish I might,
Have my wish come true tonight.

My wish was that I could see a star up close tonight," Thumper said.

"When I heard your wish, I volunteered to come," said Stella. "I've wanted to come to Earth for a long time." But the journey had clearly exhausted her. She was still very weak.

"We'll take care of you," said Willy Nilly. "Come with us. You can rest until you feel better."

Thumper reached down and helped her up. Leaning on her new friends, Stella climbed out of the crater.

The coals in Willy Nilly and Thumper's campfire were still warm. Willy Nilly reached down and fanned new sparks to reignite the blaze.

"Stella, how about a marshmallow?" Thumper asked.

"Ooh, I love marshmallows," she said. "I like mine burned with a gooey center."

Thumper gave Willy Nilly an "I told you so" look.

Stella took a vial of pink powder from her bag and sprinkled it over herself. Her cuts and bruises started to disappear.

"What is that?" Willy Nilly asked.

"It's my stardust. It fixes things and does a lot more. It's what got me here, and it's what will get me back home."

"You mean you're not staying here with us?" Thumper asked.

"I can't. I am a star in the Big Dipper, and I have to get back soon."

"But you just got here," Thumper said.

"Yes, but I belong up there. I was so excited to see Earth that I left my place in the sky without thinking about all those who depend on me. Astronomers and ship captains use the Big Dipper to find the North Star. They need the North Star to navigate."

"How will you get back?" Willy Nilly asked.

"I didn't realize gravity was so strong on Earth. If you guys can just get me to ten thousand feet, I can get some momentum," Stella said. "Can you help me?"

"Of course we'll help you, Stella," Thumper said. "We'll think of something, won't we, Willy?"

"I'm already thinking, Thump!"

Willy Nilly squinted one eye. The whiskers on his lip bunched up, and he tapped his paw rhythmically.

"How about a really big ramp?" asked Thumper. "We can borrow a car. Stella can drive really fast and launch into space when the car goes off the top."

"Won't work," said Willy Nilly. "She can't get high enough, and what happens when the car comes crashing back to the ground?"

"Then how about if we mount a small gas-fired engine onto Stella's back, and light it to propel Stella into space?" asked Thumper.

"Ummm . . . NO-o!" Stella chimed in. "That could hurt."

"I've got it," Willy Nilly said. "We'll build an airplane."

"Great idea," Thumper said. "Hey, uh, Willy, how are we going to build an airplane?"

"Let's think," Willy Nilly said. He rubbed his whiskers and squinted his eye again. "We have a really big barrel that was once used to store Hoop 'n' Holler's water supply. That would make a nice fuselage."

"Yeah, and for the wings and tail, we could use parts from that old broken windmill outside of town," Thumper said.

"We can make the propeller from the blade of the fan that used to cool the mitten factory," Willy Nilly said.

"And those old motorcycle engines in the junkyard—I bet we'll find one that still works," added Thumper. "It won't be much horsepower, but it will get Stella high enough."

"That sounds perfect, guys," said Stella, who seemed to have totally recovered from her fall. "Would it be possible to have it ready when the sun meets the horizon tomorrow night?"

"Why then?" Thumper asked.

"As soon as we see Polaris, the North Star, we need to take off," Stella said. "It's always due north, and it's the most important star in the night sky for navigation. It becomes visible at dusk. If we leave too early, I won't have Polaris to guide me. I want to return to the Big Dipper before too many navigators notice that I'm missing. If we leave too late, my home in the sky will be too hard for me to reach."

"It's just after nightfall now," Willy Nilly said. "That gives us about twenty-three hours before the plane needs to be airworthy. Let's split up and gather the materials. We can meet back at the long, flat patch of ground in the next pasture. We can take off from there."

13

They worked hard through the night, and when the sun rose the next morning, Thumper was tightening the last bolt on the second wing.

"Time to start building the tail section!" he said.

Then, out of the corner of his eye, Thumper saw something he had never seen before. "Willy! Look! What is that? It's really spooky!"

The fan blade from the mitten factory was floating two feet off the ground. It moved closer to the airplane.

"This is really weird. I've never seen a floating fan blade before!" Willy Nilly said. The blade turned and headed straight toward them.

The blade stopped. Willy Nilly and Thumper heard a chuckle.

"Don't worry, guys. It's just me," Stella's voice said.

"Stella? What's going on?" Willy Nilly asked.

"You can't see me during the daylight, just like you can't see any other stars in the sky," Stella said. "I'll sprinkle myself with some stardust. That should help after a few hours."

Stella gradually became visible again. When the sun was at its highest point in the sky, they put the final touches on the plane. It was done.

"Let's check the list," said Willy Nilly.

"I'm famished," Thumper said. "It's time for lunch!"

"Safety first, guys. We'll do this quickly so your stomach will stop growling." Willy Nilly grabbed his clipboard.

They ran through the safety checklist. Everything was ready.

"Great!" Thumper said. "Now let's eat!"

"We need to be quick so we can do a test flight," Willy Nilly said.

When they were done with their lunch, the friends walked back to the plane. Thumper and Stella were talking about their favorite foods. "Banana splits are the absolute best! I'll definitely come back to Earth for those," Stella said.

Willy Nilly, who was walking a few of steps ahead of Thumper and Stella, stopped cold in his tracks. "Stella," he asked, "when we went to lunch, did you leave your stardust in your bag, underneath the plane?"

"Why?" Stella asked. And then she saw for herself. Her bag was lying open in the dirt.

Stella stared. "Ohh, this is bad," she said. "This is worse than bad. It's disastrous. I can't go anywhere without my stardust."

"Willy, look!" Thumper said. "Here. And here. And here." There were huge footprints all around the plane. "Are you thinking what I'm thinking?" he asked.

"If what you're thinking is that those footprints belong to Gnarly and Knotty's big ugly feet, I sure am," Willy Nilly answered.

"Do you think they stole the stardust and are taking it back to Wanda the Wicked Witch?" Thumper asked.

"I *know* they are," said Willy Nilly grimly.

"Who are Wanda, and Gnarly and Knotty?" Stella asked.

"Wanda is the meanest, foulest witch in all of Choco," Willy Nilly said. "You have to be very careful if you ever meet her. Gnarly and Knotty are her henchmen. They help Wanda do her wicked work."

"They are the ugliest living beings in all of Choco," said Thumper. "Their heads are bumpy from being whacked by Wanda's broomstick."

"It won't be good for *anyone* if those three have the stardust," added Willy Nilly. "We have to get it back, and fast."

Using his canine tracking ability, Willy Nilly began to follow the huge footprints. After tracking them for more than two hours, the trio was discouraged. They knew they didn't have much time.

"Look!" Willy Nilly pointed down to the rocks underfoot, where something glinted in the sunlight.

"Those are candy wrappers," said Thumper. "They've been here!"

"And not very long ago," Stella added. "I can still smell the choco-late." The effects of the stardust were wearing off, and she was almost invisible again.

The three friends looked into the distance and saw Gnarly and Knotty high-stepping through the tall grass. "Let's go!" Willy Nilly said.

When they had almost caught up to Gnarly and Knotty, Stella held out her hand. "Guys, I've got this," she said.

Willy Nilly and Thumper watched the grass part as Stella, who was now completely invisible, made her way toward Wanda's helpers.

"Gnarly! Knotty!" Stella shouted loud and clear.

"What did you say?" Gnarly's voice reached the friends, too.

"I didn't say anything. I thought *you* said something," Knotty said, scowling at his partner in crime.

"You have something that belongs to me," Stella said, "and I want it back now."

Gnarly and Knotty turned toward Stella's voice. Fear descended over their faces because they thought they were talking to a ghost!

"Put the stardust down and walk away," Stella said firmly.

Gnarly dropped the stardust on the ground. The vial rose in the air and bobbed across the meadow as Stella ran toward her friends.

"We've got to get that vial of stardust back to Wanda or we'll be in big trouble!" Knotty said.

"Bigger than big. Huge!" replied Gnarly, and he took off after the vial with Knotty close behind.

Stella ran as fast as she could, but the henchmen ran faster. Just as they were about to reach her, she threw the stardust to Thumper. The vial soared into the air, and Gnarly and Knotty both jumped for it. Their heads collided and they fell to the ground, unconscious.

Thumper reached down and tied their shoelaces tightly together with a double knot. "That ought to slow them down for a while," he said.

"Let's go!" Willy Nilly said. The friends' shadows were long as they ran back toward the plane.

By the time the three friends had returned to the takeoff strip, the sun was almost touching the horizon.

Thumper jumped into the plane first, then grabbed hold of Stella's hand and pulled her into the plane too.

Willy Nilly jumped in, turned the plane's ignition switch to on, and pressed the starter button. Nothing. He tried again. Silence. A third time, Willy Nilly pressed the starter. The engine sputtered and stalled, sputtered and stalled. A small puff of smoke appeared below the engine.

"C'mon, *please!*" Willy Nilly said under his breath.

As if it had heard him, the engine finally sputtered into a steady roar. The propeller blades began to turn, slowly at first, then faster and faster, until finally they looked like a blur.

Willy Nilly released the brakes; the plane sped down the strip.

"Hey Willy, are we going to make it over those?" Thumper asked, pointing to a grove of trees at the end of the runway.

"I sure hope so," Willy Nilly replied. He adjusted the throttle for more speed and pulled the control stick toward him to make the plane rise. The plane lifted off and just cleared the highest branches of the tallest trees.

"Success!" Thumper said.

But they were further from success than they thought.

In the distance a dark blur was moving toward them quickly. "Is that another airplane?" Thumper asked.

"It's moving like a bird," Willy Nilly said.

"It looks to me like someone on a broomstick!" Stella said.

"It's Wicked Wanda!" all three said at the same time.

"I've got to outfly her. It's our only chance," Willy Nilly said. He adjusted the throttle again to increase the plane's power and speed. Wanda sped up, too. "Give me the stardust!" she yelled, flying so close above them that they had to duck.

"You can't have it! Leave us alone," Stella yelled back.

Willy Nilly yanked the control stick toward him, and the plane climbed steeply. Wanda climbed, too, and was soon beside them. Willy Nilly set the throttle for maximum speed, but Wanda kept right up.

"I won't ask again," she screamed.

"We won't *ever* give it to you!" Willy Nilly yelled.

"Oh, yes you will!" Wanda drew an arm out from under her cape and flung a bolt of white-hot lightning at the plane.

"I WILL DESTROY YOU!" she screeched.

The lightning struck. There was a jolt and a shudder. The left wing began to wobble and the plane began to shake. Black smoke poured from where the current had hit.

"Stella, I'll hold the plane as steady as I can, but you have to launch yourself now!" Willy Nilly said.

"We don't have enough altitude. I won't make it."

"You have to! We're going down!" Willy Nilly replied.

"No, we're not!" Stella was out of her seat. Holding tightly to the sides of the plane, she rubbed stardust across the wings and fuselage. "This should give us some more time."

The wing stopped wobbling. The plane gained altitude and began to fly faster again, but not fast enough to outfly Wicked Wanda.

"You're all dead!" she cackled as she caught up with them. "Say your good-byes!" Wanda hurled a second lightning bolt.

The friends watched in horror as the lightning headed straight for them. It made contact with the plane, but Stella's stardust had created a protective shield, so the friends felt nothing. Instead . . .

The bolt bounced back toward Wanda and slammed into her broomstick, snapping it in half!

"Force field engaged!" Thumper called out.

"Curses! You haven't seen . . . the last . . . of Wandaaaaaaaaaaaaaaa!!" the witch shouted, her voice fading away as she plummeted to Earth.

Willy Nilly took the airplane high enough to give Stella the best chance to launch herself home. Stella spread stardust all over herself.

"Ready?" Willy Nilly yelled.

"Ready!" Stella shouted back. She handed the nearly empty vial to Thumper. "This is for you guys. I'll be back for a visit, I promise!"

Stella stepped to the back of the plane. She bent her knees, then leaped into the evening air. "Look for me in the Big Dipper!" she shouted as she headed for home.

"We'll miss you," Thumper called after her.

"Be safe," Willy Nilly called, even though he knew she was already too far away to hear them.

Stella disappeared into deep space just as the last sliver of evening sun bobbed on the horizon. She would be back in place just in time for all the navigators, astronomers, and ship captains who needed her.

"It was nice of Stella to leave us the vial," Thumper said as their campfire crackled softly in the night.

"There's a tiny amount of stardust still in it. We can keep it in our treasure chest," Willy Nilly said. He stuck his marshmallow into the campfire's flames, and it caught fire.

"Hey! You don't like burned marshmallows!" Thumper said.

"I thought I'd try them again. I figure if both you and Stella like them that way, they must be good." The two best friends looked into the sky. "There it is," Willy Nilly said, pointing to the Big Dipper.

"And there *she* is," Thumper responded. "It's pretty cool knowing she'll be looking down and watching our adventures."

"I hope she'll come back soon," said Willy Nilly.

Thumper grinned. "I've already started wishing!"

Notes from Willy Nilly and Thumper's Library

WHAT IS A STAR?

A star is a huge ball of gas, mostly hydrogen and helium. There are trillions of stars—so many that we can't count them all—but most of the stars we see are those closest to Earth. Stars are so hot that they convert hydrogen into helium through a process called nuclear fusion, which gives off light and energy.

The closest star is the sun. It is 93 million miles away, and its light takes about 8.3 minutes to reach Earth. In star terms, that's close! Other stars are so far away that we measure their distance in *light-years*—that is, how many years it takes for their light to reach us. Some stars are just a few light-years away; others are thousands or millions of light-years away.

OUR SOLAR SYSTEM AND GALAXY

A solar system includes a star and everything that travels in orbit around it, such as planets, dwarf planets, and moons. Earth and seven other planets revolve around the sun. In order from closest to the sun to farthest, they are Mercury, Venus, Earth, Mars, Jupiter, Saturn, Uranus, and Neptune.

Pluto used to be considered the ninth planet, but it's been reclassified as a dwarf planet, along with Ceres, Eris, Makemake, and Haumea. Scientists believe that our solar system may have dozens more dwarf planets that haven't been discovered yet.

Our moon, which revolves around Earth, is the largest, most visible object in the night sky. But we aren't the only planet with a moon. So far scientists have discovered 178 moons in our solar system! Saturn has at least 53.

Our solar system is part of an enormous group of stars called a *galaxy*. Our galaxy is called the Milky Way.

WHAT ARE CONSTELLATIONS?

Throughout human history, people have gazed at stars twinkling in the night sky. Long ago they gave names to the patterns and shapes they saw. We call these star patterns *constellations*. Astronomers (people who study stars) say there are 88 of them.

A FEW WELL-KNOWN STARS AND CONSTELLATIONS

If you live in the northern half of the world, or Northern Hemisphere, on a clear night it's easy to see the seven stars that form a long, curved handle attached to a squarish bowl. This is a group of stars called the Big Dipper—it's part of Ursa Major (the Big Bear.)

If you trace a line upward from the bowl's two outside stars, opposite the handle, you'll find Polaris, also called the North Star. The constellation Orion, the Greek hunter and warrior, has a belt with three bright stars in it. Behind him the Big Dog (or Canis Major) frolics, and at his feet is the Hare.

WHAT ARE SHOOTING OR FALLING STARS?

They aren't really stars. They're *meteors*: streaks of light caused by bits of rock, metal, or ice that fall into Earth's atmosphere. These bits of falling matter are called *meteoroids*. As a meteoroid hurtles through the air, it heats up, melts, and vaporizes. That's why it creates a blazing streak of light against the night sky. Sometimes tens or even hundreds of meteors streak across the sky at the same time. This is called a meteor shower.

Most meteoroids burn up during their journey, but many also land on Earth every day. Once they land, they're called *meteorites*. They're usually small, anywhere from the size of a grain of sand to the size of a fist. Scientists study meteorites to learn more about the kinds of materials that exist in our solar system.

THE COMPASS IN THE SKY

The star Polaris shows which way is north for people in the Northern Hemisphere. Polaris is not visible in the Southern Hemisphere. There, travelers know which way is south by finding the constellation known as the Southern Cross.

CELESTIAL NAVIGATION

Celestial navigation is the science of figuring out where you are by looking at the sky. For thousands of years, people traveling across long distances have needed a method to find their way, especially if they were traveling by sea. Because the sun, moon, stars, and planets move in predictable patterns, ancient travelers used them as guides.

By measuring the angle between the horizon and a specific star, navigators figured out where they were and how to get where they wanted to go. Using this information, people could head out to trade and explore new lands. Instruments like the *sextant* were developed to make the task easier.

THE FIRST AIRPLANE

Before the 1900s, the dream of flying like a bird led to all kinds of inventions—big kites, strap-on wings, and "glider" planes that floated on wind currents. But no one succeeded in designing a real flying machine. Then along came two brothers from Ohio, Wilbur and Orville Wright. They invented the first engine-powered, pilot-steered plane. They flew it for the first time on December 17, 1903.

Unlike modern planes, the Wright brothers' aircraft did not have an enclosed body section, or *fuselage*. The pilot—either Wilbur or Orville—would lie on his stomach with his hips in a wooden "cradle." Wires connected the cradle to the wing tips. The pilot would slide the cradle right to turn the plane toward the right, and to the left to go left. A rudder connected to the wing tips helped keep the plane steady. The brothers' ideas about how to control a plane's movements in the air are still in use today.

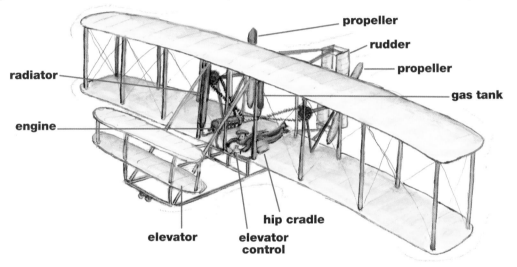

AIRPLANE SPEEDS

In a telegram home after the first flight, Orville wrote that their plane's average speed through the air was 31 miles an hour. Today the fastest single-engine planes can go over 300 miles an hour. The cruising speed of a passenger jet can top 600 miles per hour.

INTO THE MODERN FLYING AGE

By 1909 many people were flying planes. Pilots started sitting upright. By the 1920s planes began to have a single pair of wings instead of two pairs, and were made of metal, which was more durable than wood. The first modern passenger airplane, the Boeing 247, appeared in 1933. It carried 10 passengers and 3 crew members, and had an enclosed cockpit, two engines, landing gear, autopilot, and instruments for night and bad weather.

From then on, planes continued to get bigger, faster, and more comfortable for passengers. Powerful gas-turbine engines—known as *jet engines*—allowed planes to go faster than ever. Today when we ride most large commercial airplanes, they are jet aircraft.

Dedications

To my wife, Paula, the love of my life.
—J. H.

To the memory of my uncle Bill,
who taught me the power of the written word.
—J. P.

For Johann, my soul mate.
—M. v. H.

BOOKS IN THE ADVENTURES OF WILLY NILLY & THUMPER SERIES:

For more information, please visit www.willynillyandthumper.com

About the Authors

JIM HENRY is a businessman, philanthropist, and lover of adventure who first heard stories about Willy Nilly from his father. He added the character of Thumper and began telling the stories to his own children forty years ago. The tradition continues as he tells the tales to his grandchildren. A father of three and grandfather of eleven, he lives in Midland, Texas, with his wife, Paula.

JIMMY PATTERSON is an award-winning journalist, a novelist, and the author of several nonfiction books, including *A History of Character: The Story of Midland, Texas*. A father of three and grandfather of one, he lives in Midland, Texas, with his wife, Karen.

About the Illustrator

MARJORIE VAN HEERDEN has written and/or illustrated more than 120 children's picture books. Her work has won awards internationally. A mother of two and grandmother of three, she lives in Gordon's Bay, South Africa, with her husband, Johann.

BUY A BOOK

GIVE A BOOK

For each book bought in the Adventures of Willy Nilly & Thumper series, we will give a new book to an organization that serves children.

The Willy Nilly & Thumper Team

The Willy Nilly stories were told by Jim Henry, transcribed by Michele Canis, and written by Jimmy Patterson. This book was illustrated by Marjorie van Heerden and designed by Stephanie Bart-Horvath. The nonfiction notes for this book were written by Alexandra Alger. Administrative support was provided by DiAnn Barker. Janet Frick copyedited the manuscript. The project director and editor was Simone Kaplan.

The Adventures of Willy Nilly & Thumper | Book Three: Stella Star

Copyright © 2016 Willy Nilly Stories LLC | All rights reserved.

No portion of this book may be reproduced in whole or in part, by any means whatever, except for passages excerpted for purposes of review, without the prior written permission of the publisher, Willy Nilly Stories LLC.

www.willynillyandthumper.com

Design by Stephanie Bart-Horvath

Library of Congress Cataloging-in-Publication Data

Names: Henry, Jim (James Cruce), 1934- author. | Patterson, Jimmy (James Lee), 1959- author. | van Heerden, Marjorie, illustrator.

Title: Stella Star / by Jim Henry with Jimmy Patterson ; illustrated by Marjorie van Heerden.

Description: First edition. | Midland, TX : Willy Nilly Stories LLC, [2016] | Series: The adventures of Willy Nilly & Thumper ; book 3 | Following the story: "Notes from Willy Nilly and Thumper's Library": the science of stars and astronomy by Alexandra Alger. | Audience: Ages 4-8. | Summary: Willy Nilly and Thumper are best friends and adventurers with a knack for getting into tight squeezes and out of sticky situations, and always, always doing the right thing. When they meet a star who has fallen to earth, the friends are determined to return her to her place in the sky before nightfall—and before a wicked witch makes it impossible for her to return. Ever. —Publisher.

Identifiers: ISBN: 978-1-939368-09-6 (case); 978-1-939368-06-5 (pbk) | LCCN: 2016910026

Subjects: LCSH: Rabbits—Juvenile fiction. | Dogs—Juvenile fiction. | Friendship—Juvenile fiction. | Quests (Expeditions)—Juvenile fiction. | Stars—Juvenile fiction. | Witches—Juvenile fiction. | Magic—Juvenile fiction. | Adventure stories. | Children's stories. | CYAC: Rabbits—Fiction. | Dogs—Fiction. | Friendship—Fiction. | Quests (Expeditions)—Fiction. | Stars—Fiction. | Witches—Fiction. | Magic—Fiction. | LCGFT: Action and adventure fiction. / BISAC: JUVENILE FICTION / Action & Adventure / General.

Classification: LCC: PZ7.1.H466 A383 2016 | DDC: [Fic]—dc23

Printed in the United States of America

2 4 6 8 9 7 5 3 1

First Edition